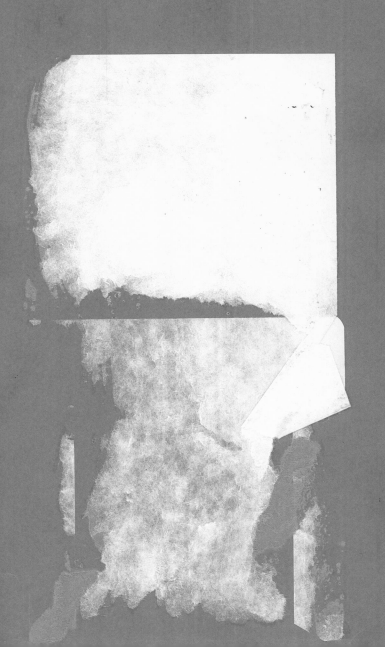

One Round Moon
and a Star for Me

A MELANIE KROUPA BOOK

One Round Moon
and a Star for Me

Story by Ingrid Mennen · *Pictures by Niki Daly*

Orchard Books   New York

One round moon.
So many stars.

A falling star, Mama!
Look how Papa catches it in his warm brown blanket.
See how it slips into his silver milk bucket.
"A star for a new baby," says Mama.

Now, Moon, please go! Go to your home.
Go sleep in your hut. Roll up night.
Look how Sun is chasing Moon, Mama.
Big round moon, back to her empty hut.

Ah! There! One round sun!
Hurry through the grass — make it gold.
Run over the hill, past Papa's herd.

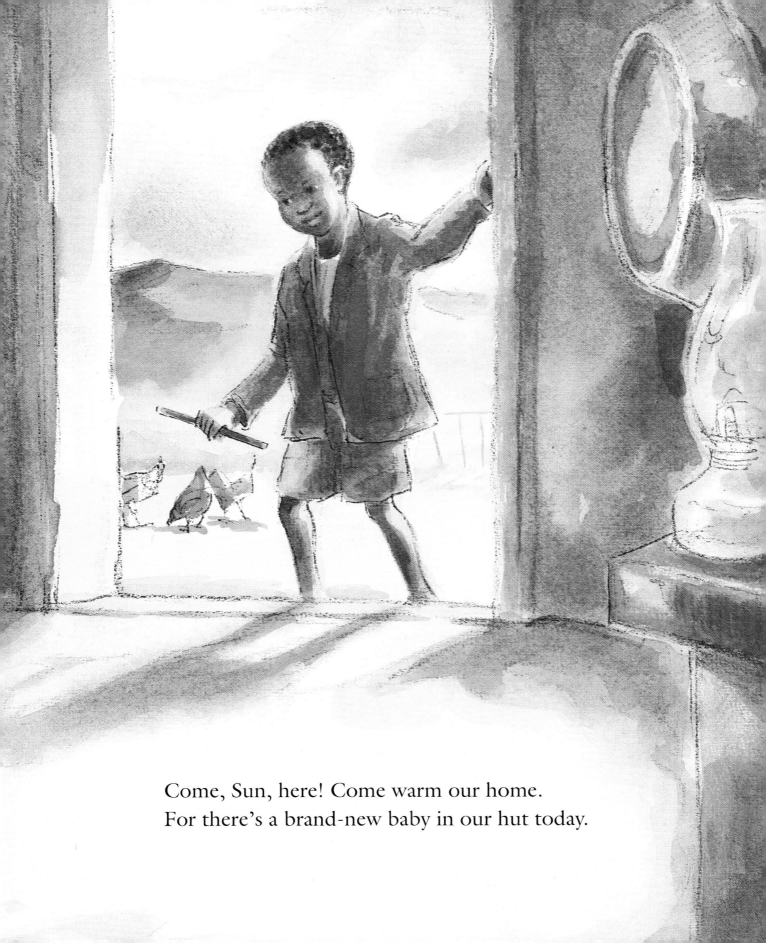

Come, Sun, here! Come warm our home.
For there's a brand-new baby in our hut today.

Mamkhulu — my aunty — lifts me high. I stick two stalks of sun yellow grass in the roof, above the door. Mamkhulu says, "Now the men will come in only when the inkaba-cord falls from the baby's belly."

Three makoties—three young girls — bring water for the baby, balancing buckets on their heads.

Sis Beauty brings a new cake of soap she has saved for so long. Sis Anna brings a little paraffin lamp made from a tin and a piece of wick-cloth to light for the baby.

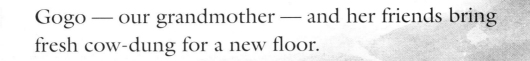

Gogo — our grandmother — and her friends bring
fresh cow-dung for a new floor.

Inside, Mama sings a tula-tula hush-hush song
to the baby.

And then Papa comes. He leaves his silver bucket, brimming with milk, at the door and kneels to look at the baby's two tiny hands.

"They look like my hands," he says.

He looks at the baby's tiny round ears.

"Mama's ears."

He unwraps the blanket, and there are two small feet with ten tiny toes.

"They will walk well." Papa nods.

"I'm the baby's father," says Papa with a smile.

We walk to the other men, but my heart feels dark,
like a night with no moon.
At last I ask, "Papa, are you really my papa too?"

He takes my hands and puts them next to his.
"See," he says. "I am really your papa too."
He looks me close in the eye. "Your eyes are like
Mama's eyes. You are your papa's child and you
are your mama's child."

He puts his arms around me and says,
"Tonight, when the moon is big and round and
the stars light up God's great sky, I'll show you,
there is also a star for you."

One round moon.

And a star for me.

For Joyce, who shares her life with me —I.M.
For Laura Cecil, my friend and agent —N.D.

Text copyright © 1994 by Ingrid Mennen   Illustrations copyright © 1994 by Niki Daly

Orchard Books, 95 Madison Avenue, New York, NY 10016

Manufactured in the United States of America. Printed by Barton Press, Inc.

Bound by Horowitz/Rae.

The text of this book is set in 16 point ITC Galliard. The illustrations are pencil and watercolor reproduced in full color.

10 9 8 7 6 5 4 3 2 1

Library of Congress Cataloging-in-Publication Data

Mennen, Ingrid.
    One round moon and a star for me / story by Ingrid Mennen ; pictures by Niki Daly.
        p.   cm.
    "A Melanie Kroupa book" — Half t.p.
    Summary: A young boy of rural Lesotho needs reassurance that his father is still his papa, too, when a new baby is born into the family.
        ISBN 0-531-06804-8. — ISBN 0-531-08654-2 (lib. bdg.)
    [1. Babies — Fiction. 2. Blacks — Lesotho — Fiction. 3. Lesotho — Fiction. 4. Fathers and sons — Fiction.]
I. Daly, Niki, ill. II. Title.
PZ7.M529On 1994
[E] — dc20   93-9628